This book belongs to

....

www.makebelieveideas.co.uk

Written by Alexandra Robinson.
Illustrated by Clare Fennell.

THE UNICORNS

are coming to town

Clare Fennell ★ Alexandra Robinson

make
believe
ideas

One bright and merry *Christmas Eve,*
Santa planned a treat.
He booked the *Unicorn Ice Spa*
for his faithful *reindeer fleet.*

The
Ice
Spa

Reception

Excitedly, they went inside
to start their *pamper day*.
They dressed in gowns and fluffy socks,
then dashed to the *buffet*.

The **unicorns** were mega fans
of **Santa's reindeer crew.**
So, having them as special guests
made all their **dreams** come true.

They welcomed in the V.I.Ps,
greeting them with awe,
then served them up their *buffet feast,*
with snacks and treats galore.

Throughout the day, the reindeer team were pampered to the max.

This is the life!

They chilled out in the *tinsel tub*,

Glitter

Hoof Shine Station

with snow masks to *relax*.

Inside the *Ice Spa Hair Salon,*
they had a snow shampoo.

Their fur was dried and *filled* with *gems,*
plus *bells* and *baubles,* too!

And though the *jewels* were *everywhere,*
the *deer* kept wanting *more.*

Soon, their coats were so *bejewelled,*

they couldn't see the floor!

Before long, *Santa's sleigh team* had to leave for Christmas Town.

These jewels weigh a ton!

Hope to see you soon!

The glitzy *reindeer* called their jet and packed their dressing gowns.

The reindeer knew the unicorns would love to watch their *flight*.

They said: "We've got some extra seats — come join us for tonight."

When the *unicorns* arrived,
the *elves* gave them a tour.
They marvelled at the *toy parade*
and giant *chocolate store.*

Wow!

CHOCOLATE STORE

The clock struck eight, and it was time
for *Santa's team* to go.
So, everybody *marched* uphill
to watch the *Sleigh Launch Show.*

SWEETS 'N' TREATS

But when the deer put on their reins,
the straps began to break,
and the extra jingly-jangly bells
just made their poor heads ache.

And as they jumped for takeoff,
their jewelled coats weighed them down.
They howled,

"We'll never pull the sleigh –
we can't leave Christmas Town!"

Ouch!

The *elves* and *snowmen* tried to help
with tiny combs and tools.
But all the *bells* were *stuck* in place,
and so were all the *jewels!*

The reindeer team felt *helpless*, but then one cried out with *glee*:

That's a good idea!

"The unicorns could fly the sleigh, if they will all agree?"

The **unicorns** looked doubtful –
they'd *never flown* a sleigh.

"You can do it," said the deer.
"Trust yourselves today!"

The brave, excited unicorns all nodded with delight:

"We'll try our best, and use our horns to guide you through the night."

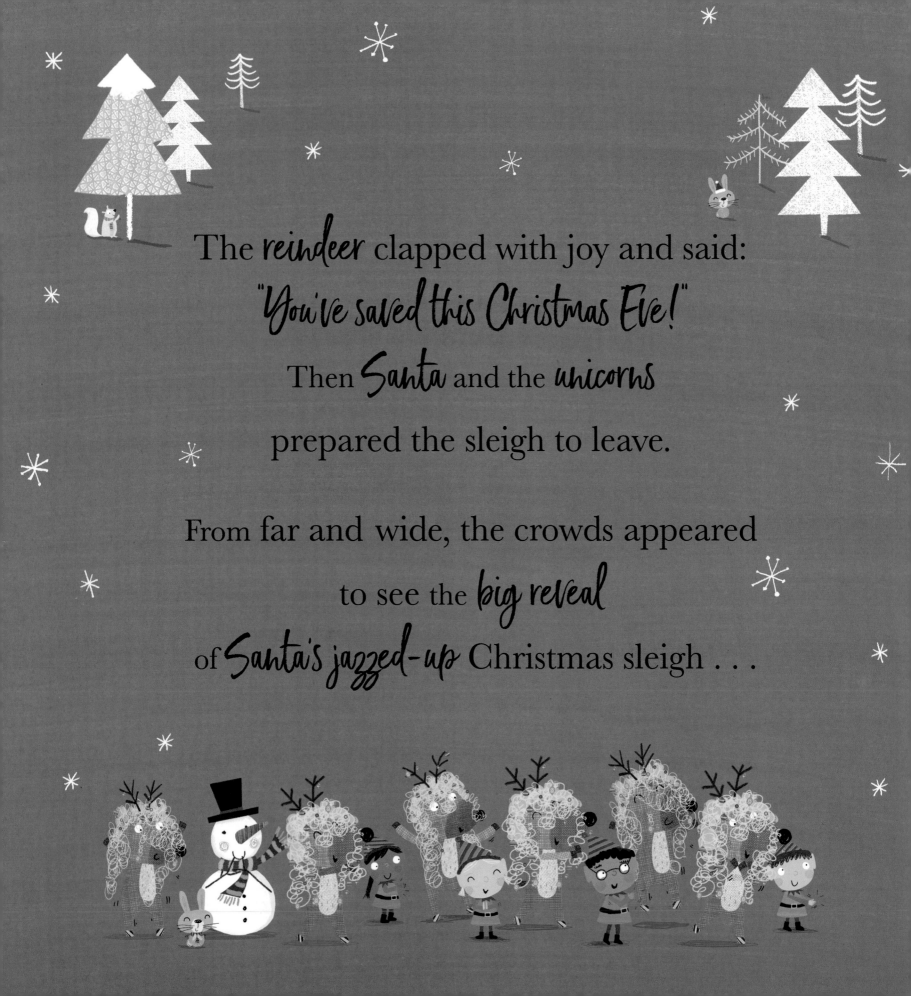

The reindeer clapped with joy and said:
"You've saved this Christmas Eve!"
Then Santa and the unicorns
prepared the sleigh to leave.

From far and wide, the crowds appeared
to see the big reveal
of Santa's jazzed-up Christmas sleigh . . .

...with a **rainbow steering wheel!**

The next day, all the unicorns received a gold rosette.

They'd won a North-Pole record for the fastest sleigh ride yet!